Three friends . . . one mission

For Noah, Sera, and JiJi, the Starseeker
space station is called home. The universe
is their classroom. And homework
involves learning to float in zero gravity!

These friends have joined the
Starseeker training program. And life as
they know it will never be the same.

In loving memory of Commander Dominic John Grasso,
USNR, Retired, and the long friendship we shared.
His belief in space flight and exploration was
a great inspiration.
—D.B.

To Bernette, Gina, Kimberly, and Edie
for helping us launch Starseeker.
—E.R. & D.B.

Copyright © 2000 by Elaine Raphael and Don Bolognese.
All rights reserved. Published by Scholastic Inc.
2050: VOYAGE OF THE STARSEEKER, SCHOLASTIC, CARTWHEEL BOOKS and associated logos are trademarks and/or registered trademarks of Scholastic Inc.

Library of Congress Cataloging-in-Publication Data

Raphael, Elaine.
    Asteroid alert / by Elaine Raphael and Don Bolognese.
      p.   cm.— (2050, Voyage of the Starseeker)
    Summary: In 2050 Noah, Sera, and Jiji experience both excitement and fear as they embark on their assignment aboard Starseeker, a space station designed to find and destroy large asteroids endangering the Earth.
    ISBN 0-439-07815-6
    [1. Science Fiction.] I. Bolognese, Don. II. Title. III. Series
PZ7.R1812As 2000
[Fic] — dc21
                                       99-16495
                                         CIP

12 11 10 9 8 7 6 5 4 3 2 1   00 01 02 03 04 05 06

Printed in the U.S.A.   24

First printing, January 2000

2050

VOYAGE OF THE STARSEEKER™

BOOK 1
ASTEROID ALERT

**ELAINE RAPHAEL &
DON BOLOGNESE**

SCHOLASTIC INC.
New York Toronto London Auckland Sydney
Mexico City New Delhi Hong Kong

For many years,
the people of Earth
have lived in fear.

Fear that a huge mass of rock and ice from space — an asteroid — might strike their planet. Fear that, just like the dinosaurs millions of years before, they would be destroyed.

Now the people have a new hope.

To protect Earth, the United Space Agency has built a space station called Starseeker. Like a man-made planet, Starseeker will orbit the sun. Its mission is to find and destroy large asteroids that are a danger to Earth.

Noah, Sera, and JiJi are members of the station's training program. Noah, age 14, will be a back-up pilot for one of Starseeker's many patrol ships. Sera, age 12, will be a lab assistant studying asteroids. And JiJi, age 9, will assist her mother in the station's animal laboratory.

On January 6, 2050, these three friends will board Starseeker from their base on Earth's moon. Together with a crew of over 300 scientists and astronauts, they will embark on the adventure of their lives. . . .

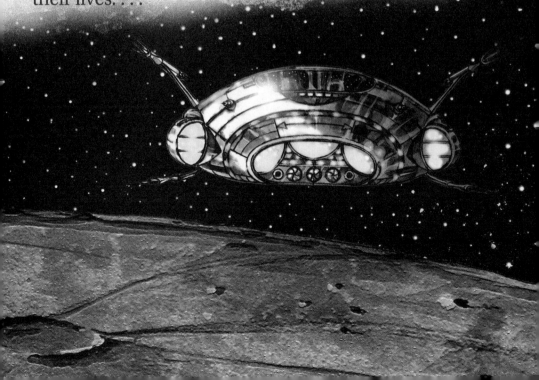

1 A FRIEND IN NEED

time • Three days to Starseeker launch
place • The Moon

Earth shone brightly against the
star-filled sky. The planet's blue glow lit the
spaceship as it landed on the moon's surface.

Noah dropped to the ground through the
ship's lower hatch. He waved to the captain
and watched as the small craft rose into the
darkness.

As he headed toward his friend Sera, Noah's
space boots crunched silently on the moon's
rocky surface. Sera was so busy studying a
crater ledge, she didn't see him coming.

"Some scientist you'll make." It was Noah's voice, laughing in her headset. "You don't even notice a person standing right next to you!"

Sera smiled as she stood up. "What are you doing here? I thought you were taking your flight test." Then she added with a grin, "You didn't crash the ship already, did you?"

"I passed!" Noah announced. "I'm an official cadet pilot."

"Wow!" said Sera. "That's great! What's your assignment?"

"I'm part of the Asteroid Research Project," Noah answered. "I'll be a back-up pilot on Captain Ryan's team."

"I'm on that project, too," Sera said as she picked up an instrument. "See this laser scanner? In seconds, it can tell me an asteroid's age — and what it's made of!"

Noah smiled at his friend's enthusiasm. Sera was very serious about her work. That was why her parents had let her come on this mission alone while they worked on their own space station near Mars.

As they headed back to Moonbase Central, Noah asked, "Can people survive on an asteroid? Could they find any water there?"

Sera thought for a moment. "Let's see," she said. "An asteroid is a lot like the moon — only much smaller. Of course there's no air, so a

person would need a supply of oxygen to breathe. There's not much gravity, but there could be water in the form of ice. I guess it's possible," she answered, "but it wouldn't be easy. Why do you ask?"

Before Noah could answer, a message sounded in his headset. A practice drill on space rescue was beginning in five minutes.

"I'd better hurry," said Noah as their rover entered the base's docking area.

He seemed grateful for the interruption in their conversation. "You know how Captain Simon gets when someone's late."

Sera watched as Noah raced off. *What were those questions all about?* she wondered.

"Hi, Noah," Sera said as they met in the main hall later that day. "That must be an exciting class."

"You're right, Sera, space rescue is really dangerous. That's why these drills are —"

"Look," Sera interrupted, "there's JiJi."

"JiJi? Who's JiJi?" Noah asked.

"A friend I met the other day after a biology class," Sera answered. "Her mom is Dr. Wu, the head of the Animal Lab."

Noah watched as JiJi walked toward them. He couldn't help but laugh as she bounced high in the air with each step.

"Don't laugh, Noah," Sera whispered. "Remember when we still had our Earth legs the first time we came to the moon? It's not easy to walk in low gravity."

"Hi, Sera," JiJi said in a quiet voice.

"JiJi," said Sera, "this is my friend, Noah. He's going to be a back-up pilot on the space station. Noah, this is JiJi."

As Noah said hello, a monkey peeked out from behind JiJi's shoulder. It chattered happily and reached for Noah's hand.

"That's Ping," said JiJi shyly. "He's one of the animals from my mom's project."

"JiJi is going to assist her mother in the animal laboratory on the station," Sera told Noah.

"Yes," said JiJi, "but . . ." She looked as though she were about to cry.

"But what?" asked Noah.

"It's weightlessness," Sera said, putting an arm around her young friend. "JiJi was sick to her stomach the entire trip from Earth."

"If I can't show that I can handle weightlessness, I won't be allowed to go on the mission," JiJi said sadly. "My mother says I'll have to stay on Earth with my grandparents."

"Don't worry," said Noah. "We'll help you."

Just then, Ping jumped into Noah's arms.

"Ping likes you, Noah," JiJi said. And she smiled for the first time in a long while.

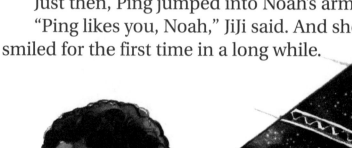

THE STARDOME

time • Two days to Starseeker launch
place • Stardome Training Station

The next morning, Sera, Noah, and JiJi took a shuttle to the astronaut training center, the Stardome. It orbited high above the moon.

Inside the dome, JiJi looked up. The blackness of the universe was all around her.

This is so different from Earth, JiJi thought. *I miss the blue sky and white clouds.*

"Are you ready, JiJi?" Sera asked softly.

JiJi didn't feel ready, but she nodded. Hand in hand, the three friends stepped off the catwalk.

Noah looked at JiJi. "It's okay," he said. "You can open your eyes."

JiJi did as Noah said and immediately wished she hadn't. Her stomach turned upside down as she watched red, blue, and gold rings float past her. Noah caught one of the rings.

"To show you can handle zero gravity," he said, "you have to collect ten of these rings in one hour."

It looks easy, JiJi thought. But each time she tried to catch a ring, she lost control. *Where is up?* she wondered. *Where is down?*

The stars seemed to spin faster and faster. JiJi grew dizzier and dizzier and her stomach began to feel sick. As a rope drifted past her, she grabbed it and held on tight.

Sera came to her. "That's all right," she said. "You'll get it. Do you want to try again?"

JiJi started to say no. Then she remembered what her grandfather always told her: she was his "beautiful moonchild." *But,* she thought, *what kind of a moonchild gets sick in space?*

"Look, JiJi," Noah called out. "My breath is like a rocket thruster." Noah blew hard and floated away like a swimmer doing the backstroke.

JiJi didn't laugh. Each time she tried to let go of the rope, she got scared and grabbed for it again.

"Sera," said Noah suddenly, "do you think you can work with JiJi alone for a while? I . . . I have a training flight to go to. It was added to the schedule this morning. I'll be back soon."

"No problem," Sera said as she turned back to JiJi. "Okay, let's take a break."

A short while later, Noah returned. He
had a big smile, and peeking out from behind
him was . . .

"Ping!" JiJi shouted. "My Ping!"

JiJi's pet floated a few feet from her,
chattering as loud as he could. He had a ring
in each paw.

JiJi reached out for her pet. She was so happy to see him that she forgot her fear. Her feet left the walkway and she floated easily to Ping. He gave her one of the rings.

"For me?" JiJi laughed. "Thanks, Ping."

"Now you only need nine more," said Sera, smiling.

JiJi looked around. She didn't feel sick. She didn't feel dizzy. "I did it!" she cried. "I let go!"

Before long, the three friends and Ping were soaring through the dome. JiJi collected her ten rings in no time.

"That was a great idea, Noah," Sera whispered as they watched JiJi play with Ping. "I knew you didn't have a flight today!"

"Well, I did . . . sort of," Noah grinned. "Let's call it: 'Professor Ping's Guide to Flying Upside Down.'"

The group left the Stardome and rode the shuttle to Moonbase. All the way back, they talked about the next day — the day their lives on the Starseeker space station would finally begin.

3 NOAH'S SECRET

time • Three months into Starseeker's mission
place • Starseeker dining hall

"Hey, Noah! JiJi!" Sera shouted. "I got a message from my parents!"

Noah and JiJi looked up from their lunch to see their friend bounding toward them.

"What did they say?" JiJi asked excitedly. She knew how much Sera missed her mother and father. JiJi couldn't imagine being millions of miles away from her mother.

"They're going to try to come here!" Sera said, her eyes shining. "They may be able to visit when our orbit brings us near their space station."

"That's great!" JiJi said. She and Sera quickly began to make plans for the visit. But, after a few minutes, they realized that Noah was silent.

"Noah," Sera said softly, "what's wrong?"

"It's nothing," Noah said, shaking his head. "It's just all this talk about parents. I can't help but think of . . ."

Sera and JiJi knew nothing about Noah's parents. He never talked about them.

JiJi put a hand on Noah's shoulder. "What is it, Noah?" she asked.

Noah took a deep breath. "Three years ago," he began, "my parents were lost on a mission to Mars. One minute they were talking to Moonbase. Then a huge solar flare knocked out their signal."

"Oh, Noah," Sera whispered. "How awful."

"When the storm was over," Noah continued, "the signal was gone and so were they. Without a signal, a search was useless." Noah looked out at the sea of stars around them. "Maybe I'm crazy, but I still believe they might be alive out there . . . somewhere."

Sera looked at Noah. "You're not crazy," she said. "They could be alive."

Somehow, hearing Sera's words made Noah feel better. *Maybe there is hope,* he thought.

Then a loud voice over the intercom broke the silence.

"Attention all crew members. Yellow alert. Intense asteroid activity. Report to your stations."

"This sounds serious," said Noah. "We'd better hurry!"

In minutes, Noah and Sera reported to their station on the flight deck. JiJi had taken Ping to her mother's laboratory.

"Attention, crew," the commander's voice echoed over the intercom. "Our orbit is taking us through an uncharted asteroid field. It covers a large area. We're going to need every patrol ship. Stand by."

Captain Ryan joined Noah and Sera.

"Noah," said the captain, "you heard the commander. We need every pilot — that includes back-up pilots. Are you up to it?"

Noah didn't hesitate. "Yes, Captain!" he said. "What are my orders?"

"We're getting some strange signals from one of the asteroids," said the captain. "I want you to get a closer look at it. Sera, we'll need some good rock data. Grab your equipment and report to Noah's ship immediately."

Three minutes later, Noah was going through his final pre-launch check. He had trained a long time for this moment and he was ready — at least, he hoped he was ready. For some reason, his stomach felt as though he had swallowed a whole net full of butterflies.

Next to him, Sera was setting up her scanning equipment. Their ship, ARC 017, was ready for take-off.

Captain Ryan's voice over the radio filled the cockpit. "ARC 017. Begin launch sequence."

"Roger," Noah answered, "all systems green."

Sera buckled herself into her seat. "Good luck," she said to Noah.

"Thanks," Noah answered. "I'll need it," he added under his breath.

"Outer doors open," said Captain Ryan. "Counting…5…4…3…2…1."

ARC 017 flew down the launch tube. Noah's knuckles were white as he gripped the controls. Looking over at Sera, he was surprised to see her eyes shut tight. *Well,* he thought, *at least I'm not the only one who's scared.*

In seconds, their ship was thousands of meters into space. Noah searched his radar for the target. The computer called out the distance to the mysterious asteroid.

"Sera, I know we're still far away," said Noah, "but can you tell its size?"

"It's pretty big, Noah," Sera answered. "I'd say maybe 30 kilometers long and 12 kilometers wide. But I need to get a closer look."

Noah increased the ship's speed. The radar image grew larger.

"That's great!" said Sera. "Now I'm getting a much better reading. Wow! This is so weird."

Noah looked at Sera's scanner screen. "What's weird?" he asked.

"Look," Sera said, pointing to the screen. "These are traces of the usual asteroid features: ice, iron, nickel." She moved her finger across

the image. "But see these lines? Those metals are not usually found on asteroids. They're man-made."

"Man-made?" said Noah. "How can that be?" He wouldn't let himself say what his mind — and his heart — were already wondering. Could this have anything to do with his parents?

Sera guessed at what Noah was thinking. "We've got to get closer," she said. "Let's go!"

4 RED ALERT!

time • 43 minutes into Noah's mission
place • 50 km from the mysterious asteroid

Noah's heart pounded in his chest as he carefully moved the ship toward the asteroid. Sera's eyes were glued to the scanner screen.

"Red alert! All stations! Red alert!" The commander's voice made both Noah and Sera jump.

Noah aimed his long-range radar in the direction of the space station. "Look!" Noah cried. "Starseeker's in danger!"

"That asteroid cluster," Sera gasped, pointing to the radar screen. "It's huge! And it's headed right for the station."

"Sera, we've got to get back to base," said Noah.

Sera looked at her friend. "But what about this weird asteroid?" she asked. "We can't just forget about it."

"We're not going to," said Noah. "I'm launching a robot probe to the asteroid; then we can track it." Noah watched as the probe sped towards its target.

A few seconds later Sera called out, "It landed, Noah. I have a signal!"

Noah looked one last time at the mysterious asteroid. *I promise I'll be back,* he said to himself. Then he changed the ship's course for Starseeker.

The commander's voice came on again. "Asteroid contact with Starseeker in thirty seconds," he said. "Seal all hatches. Starseeker switching to survival mode. Report all hits and air leaks immediately."

Noah sped his ship toward the space station. Sera followed the course of the asteroid cluster on the radar screen.

"Noah," she said, her eyes wide with fear, "the station is right in the middle of the asteroids' path. I don't think they can get out of the way in time."

The space station countdown continued. "Impact in five seconds…4…3…2…1."

Noah and Sera held their breath as the asteroids slammed into Starseeker. They heard the blare of alarms through their radio. Then the commander's voice spoke again.

"All levels!" he shouted. "Damage report!"

Noah and Sera listened as each section of the space station called in.

"Level 2, section A — 3 air leaks; auto seal has been activated."

"Hanger deck — automatic sensors off-line; switching to manual override."

"Level 1, section B . . . damage to animal lab."

"Hey," said Sera, "that's Dr. Wu speaking.
I hope JiJi and Ping are okay."

Dr. Wu's frightened voice sounded over the
radio. "Section B has broken off. Repeat.
Section B has separated from Starseeker!"

"Oh, no!" cried Sera. "JiJi's in section B."
She looked at the radar screen in horror. "Noah,
they're spinning away from the station!"

"Attention, all pilots!" the commander
ordered over the speaker. "Return to base to
organize rescue mission."

Noah stared at the radar screen. "We're the closest ship, Sera," he said. "We can't leave JiJi now. She needs us."

"But we'll be disobeying an order!" Sera cried. "The commander said — "

"I know what he said," Noah interrupted. "But if we don't go after JiJi, she could be lost forever . . . just like my parents."

Sera stopped and stared at her friend. "You're right," she said. "We have to try."

Noah pointed to a speck on the long-range radar. "There she is," he said, changing the ship's course. He raised the engines to full power.

"Don't worry, JiJi," Noah whispered. "We're coming . . ."

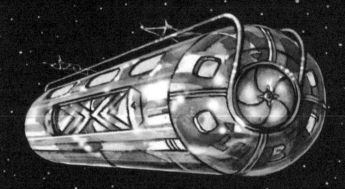

To be continued . . .